Jyoti Meditation for Children

by **Rajinder Singh**

Illustrations by Michael Schulbaum

Blooming Buds Children's Books
Radiance Publishers

Naperville, Illinois, USA
ISBN: 978-0-918224-81-1

Library of Congress Control Number: 2011905729

Foreword

Dear Parents and Teachers,

Meditation is the method used throughout the ages to re-identify with our soul and to discover the love, joy, and peace within. Whether it is called concentration, inversion, prayer, or meditation, it is a way to gain knowledge of the spiritual treasures.

Our soul shines with a brilliance greater than many suns. What power and luminosity it has! *Jyoti* is a Hindi word that means light. In Jyoti meditation we focus our attention by gazing within to contact the light already within us. It is something everyone, from a child to an elderly person, can learn.

Had we been taught how to focus our attention within during our youth, it would have become a habit by now. We would be able to do it at will anytime we wanted, but it is never too late. By learning to meditate, we can perfect the art of directing our attention to the source of happiness within us.

By practicing Jyoti meditation, we will find great rewards and benefits. First, our concentration naturally improves. We then can direct our attention to focus on anything we wish, such as our studies, our sports, our hobbies, or in solving problems. This concentrated effort helps us excel in any area we choose. I have seen many young people who have been practicing meditation rise to the top of their class. Meditation has also been proven to reduce stress, naturally enhancing the health of the body and mind.

There is yet another aspect of meditation which will have untold benefits in our lives. As the soul experiences its relationship with God, it sees each living thing—whether human, animal, or plant—as a part of God. We begin to see God's light shining in all. We begin to love all people equally and consider them part of our own family.

This world was meant to be a haven of bliss. By practicing Jyoti meditation, we are making a positive contribution to society and helping to bring about the fulfillment of this noble dream.

—Rajinder Singh

Happiness, love, joy, and peace are inside you. Through Jyoti meditation you can discover the spiritual gifts within.

To meditate, sit in a pose that is comfortable. You can sit on a chair, a sofa, or on the floor. You can even meditate lying down. Be careful you don't fall asleep and miss the beautiful wonders inside!

Close your eyes gently, just as you do when you go to sleep. Then, look into the middle of whatever you see in front of you as if you were waiting for a movie to begin.

While gazing sweetly within, slowly repeat a name of God you love. Repeat it in your mind and

not out loud. Repeating a name of God keeps your attention focused on looking within.

You may see flashes of light or circles of light. This light could be golden, yellow, orange, pink, red, blue, green, purple, violet, or white.

Enjoy the spiritual experience within you.

When you are finished meditating,
open your eyes.

Jyoti meditation fills us with inner peace, happiness, and joy, and helps us spread peace throughout our planet. These are the gifts we receive through meditation.

Helpful Hints

Jyoti meditation can be practiced anywhere. Choose a quiet place where you can meditate each day.

You may read a spiritual story or sing a spiritual song before meditation. This creates a calm feeling so it is easier to concentrate.

Once you begin meditating at the same time daily, you won't want to miss it!

Try adding a minute each time you sit. The longer you meditate, the more treasures you can discover inside.

Inner peace helps us in everything we do—our school, our sports, and our hobbies. Through Jyoti meditation we increase our peace and joy.

Children's books by Rajinder Singh

Jyoti Meditation for Children
Journey of the Phoenix
The King's Mascot

Other books by the author

Inner and Outer Peace through Meditation
Ecology of the Soul and Positive Mysticism
Education for a Peaceful World
Empowering Your Soul through Meditation
Spiritual Pearls for Enlightened Living
Silken Thread of the Divine
Visions of the New Millennium